For Those Who Fall In Love

Stories that will make you live them

Rahul v Bhole

pencil

ISBN 978-93-5458-267-7

Published in India 2021 by Pencil

A brand of
One Point Six Technologies Pvt. Ltd.
123, Building J2, Shram Seva Premises,
Wadala Truck Terminal, Wadala (E)
Mumbai 400037, Maharashtra, INDIA
E connect@thepencilapp.com
W www.thepencilapp.com

Author biography

A student of the **NATIONAL INSTITUTE OF FASHION TECHNOLOGY**, Rahul started writing eight years ago as a hobby that shaped itself into an everlasting passion.

He grew a fondness for Romanticism and Love that reflects in his work beautifully. Apart from writing, he is an avid Photographer with interests in Fashion and Wildlife. Also, he is a musician by passion.

After his Debut book "***Yaadein***", Which is a collection of poems, he is all set to present you with another surprise of love.

Romance, as a genre, is something that has intrigued him and his imagination.

It helps him create a world with his characters in a way he likes.

Another book by him is ***LOVE & ALL ABOUT IT*** is a collection of Romantic poems that will take you through a roller coaster of emotions.

CONTENTS

Epigraph

"Love finds you in the most unexpected places

& in the most unexpected ways.
So be ready, because,
Love has no season and no reason........It just happens."

Preface

Love is something you can never define. The human tendency and nature are to find someone compatible with you and strike a chord just like that, without any efforts, but the struggle starts after realising that feelings have Started to make their way into your heart and mind.

Sometimes chance encounters, sometimes childhood friends, mutual contacts, there are numerous ways people meet every day, and somehow, someone out there gets lucky every day to meet someone they were looking for until now.

Love stories are never just a figment of imagination, they might be for you, but someone out there might relate to your story because he has experienced it.

To help people relate to incidents that sometimes lead to a lifelong partnership is the main aim of this book.

Short stories leave a lasting impact and help people connect more with them, so read out what it has to narrare.

Love is the tool that can heal hearts, it is the tool that can help turn lives around, and it is a tool that can fit into anyone life without them even realising it for quite some time.

The stories in this book- "For Those Who Fall In Love", make you realise that bonds are, formed magically. People can heal from emotional breakdowns. Conveying emotions is not restricted to languages and many more.

Happy reading. I hope you like the book.

Acknowledgements

A writer is never complete without getting support from people who believe in them. The same goes for me. I want to thank some special people who have been a pillar of support and motivated me constantly to do my best.

Firstly, a big thanks to my **Mom & Dad**, who has always supported my work. They never doubted my ability or questioned my passion for writing.

Friends always play a huge role in motivating you towards your goal, and I would like to take this moment to thank them for the unconditional and rigid support that kept me going all this time.

Shalini; Prerna Gupta; Jagdish; Twinkle Lalwani; Himani Chauhan; Twisha, Ashi; Ishita; Dishant and Shamaand many more.

My Elder brothers **Sameer & Anshul**have always

supported me and helped me write better with their constant inputs and feedbacks.

My sisters, **Dhanashree & Medhavi**who have constantly pushed me and help me succeed in my endeavours.

These stories are a result of imaginations and a will to narrate stories in my way.
Along with some real-life stories from friends and strangers that added up to the flavour of the book.

This book brings out what love can do and how it can transform your life for the better.

Introduction

Love is something hard to define. The human tendency is to find someone who is compatible and ready to align with you, accept you and be with you for the way you are. Finding someone like that is a blessing or, should I say, a dream come true. Stories make us realize how chance encounters change into a lifelong affection, How friends who have known each other for years realize that they are more than just friends & how from enemies/strangers, two people come close enough and never part ways again.
Love stories are not just a figment of the imagination, and they are the proof of varied colours that your heart carries within it.

"FOR THOSE WHO FALL IN LOVE"presents you with a bunch of short romantic encounters.
Some of them, apprehended from real-life situations, from people I know, and some of them just another coloured canvas from my imagination.

I will leave it up to you to decide which one is real and which is fictional because when you read, you connect, and

you realize that all of them could be you, but when and where is all that matters.
Let Love find its way to you as you read them and drop your feedback, comments to me on **rahul.bhole@nift.ac.in**or my Instagram page - **@inked_heights_**
Moreover, let me know which story connected you the most.

Enjoy this wild ride of Love & Romance that will take you through a varied range of characters and make you live every word as you read.

RAHUL V. BHOLE

ALWAYS BUT NOT FOREVER

"You still like me"? She asked
He was spellbound and at a loss for words, but being on a video call, there was no point in hiding the fact that he still had feelings.

"Well Yeah, He replied with a Blush.
With their friendship dating back to 8 years, she might not have felt the same for him, but it was always there. Just hidden in a corner but never opening up. Although he did point it out a few times, drop a hint, but it went unnoticed.
"You are so persistent," She said in disbelief.
"Well, Persistent, not forceful," he said and smiled.
That was a point when she was silent and, even though she wanted to say something, her words refused to Come out.
"Wise talk she said with a smile, but yes, you are right."

He grinned and was about to say something when she interrupted.
"But wait, she said. "You know you should keep an open approach to everything. You can't hang on to someone even not being sure of what will happen".
He was as always ready with a reply to which even she didn't have a counter.
"Dear, life as is uncertain, Relationship, is just a chance and things change. So if it's a chance to see what the future

holds for us? I will take it. Positive or negative whatever the outcome is, I am open to it". She Blushed......

"The best part about you, she said, is that you never pushed your feelings on me."
"Get over it, he Snapped, I never will, and feelings are a necessity from both sides. If they are not, then it won't work."

"Hmmm...., you have gained knowledge sitting at home". She said and, both of them burst into laughter. Although he never made it obvious, his love for her was not just Attraction. It was a forever thing.
But as they say, some things are meant not to be, even if they are.

THE DOOR BELL

"You are a bit too far away," she said,
holding a photo frame over a call.

"Really? and what if I am closer to you than you know?" He asked.

"I wish it were possible she murmured in a low voice, and that smile faded away just like a flower loses its shine when deprived of sunshine for a prolonged period.

"Well, let's make your dream come true," he said.

She could barely understand what he said but,
the sound of her doorbell ringing made her heart skip a beat.

HOW DO I SAY

With Thoughts, I'm my mind, words in my heart.
Everything came to a standstill when I saw her pass me for the first time.

For a hundredth time today,

The silent and sober me trying to catch a glimpse of her from a mile away, looked away just when she turned towards me.

That tingling sensation, that heartthrob, those goosebumps, everything mixed with my legs wobbling, I got up and started walking away yet again.

But this time, someone held my hand.
You are so shy, said a sweet voice, and I knew who it was.
I stood there, transfixed but dare not turn to face her.

She sensed it. Pulling me towards herself, holding my cheeks in her hand gave a peck on my lips.

Walk me home, She said. Slipping her hand in mine as the tea stall behind us continued playing the song - 'Tu hai wahi.

THE FIRST DATE

I was a bit tensed and more confused. Why?
Well, the reason was that I was on my first official date with a girl. Sounds too weird for a 22-year-old to be on a first date? But, that's the fact.
I sat there sipping my cold coffee which, was the only company for the time being.

I looked around to see if she had arrived and, She was there on the gates of the cafe dressed up in a Black leather jacket on a white casual shirt which perfectly complemented, with the dark blue skirt that ran down to just above her thighs. A pair of ankle-high boots made her look even taller than her original height. I stood up just as her eyes spotted me and, I passed a smile while waving my hand. She smiled back and walked towards me. My mind was having bundles of thoughts as she approached me.

Hi, I said finally, pulling out the chair for her to sit.
"That's so sweet," she said and, to my surprise, gave a smile that blew me away.
Finally meeting you, I said. It's been a long wait.
"Honestly, speaking, same here," she said.
I was skeptical if she would like me or not, but it was going well with her.
"So how are you"? she inquired, adjusting her hairs.

"I am tensed, with the fact that it's my first date," I replied with a bit of hesitation.
"Seriously"? she looked at me with a surprised look.
"Yup," I said, taking a sip of my coffee.
"It's obvious that you are," she said with a sly smile.
"Why is that so"? I asked, looking at her.
"The fact that you are trying to have a sip of coffee from a cup that is empty helps a lot," she said and giggled.
I had no option but to laugh at my silly behaviour.

"You are by far the most modest guy I think I have talked to date," she said and, my spine felt a blot of shock as I felt her fingers curling up on mine. I looked up at her and, she was blushing, but I knew mine was more evidently visible.

I was in love with that girl.

THE FIRST MEET

I met her during an inter-college fest and, that was the moment her smile imprinted in my mind.
Somehow I found her on social media platforms and, we had a chat before I asked her to attend a party organized by our college. Although she had plans, she said, "I will try."
I had little hopes but, she did show up there and, I was yet again speechless.
There she was, clad in a black dress, complemented by a pair of heels and, of course, her evergreen smile.

My eyes had a glow that was hard to hide and didn't go unnoticed even by one of her friends.
She pulled me aside and asked, "Do you want to spend time with her alone"?
I was surprised, but I knew that my secret was secret no more and said: "I would love that."
She smiled, pushed me towards her, and said, "You guys carry on, but we will join in sometime."

There we were, standing face to face with music in the background and our moves synchronizing with it.
I had my moment and, without wasting it, I held out my hand, which she took with a smile and, my world went on a standstill mode.

She stepped close and, with her hands resting on my shoulders, my hands pulled her close and, she smiled.
We were in a moment I never wanted to let go of but repeat itself over and over again.

It was the first time I was so close to someone and, I could feel my heart pumping with such a great force that it made me shiver. The world went blurred and, she was the only one in focus for me.

That moment was Special and, I love it even today.
I don't know if she realizes that I still crave for that moment to be repeated every day.
I have been in life from the day we met and, it's hard to explain in words what she means.

That is how I met her. That is my story.

DAWN OF LOVE

Standard - 8th
Year -2009

She was my first crush.
She was what we used to call "The first love."
My life was good, but meeting her was exceptional, and it made me realize what a girl means in your life.

I was always organized, had my shirt tucked in, never missed my tie, and hairs combed perfectly.
She knew me and was the one who never let my tie out of place, never left my hairs in a ruff after sports, and even though sections were different, we were always together.

They say, "realizations come late, and when I had to leave suddenly, it was then I realized that Something was slipping off behind me, but it took time, and by the time I realized it, a year passed away.
We lost contact, and things faded away. Feelings were present, just like the sun is there always, but darkness prevents you from looking beyond it.

Those vent up feelings came all flashing back in 2017 when I met her on social media again, numbers exchanged, calls and texts started, we came close, and I could feel the

darkness fading away, but as they say -
" Something that you want so badly is never meant to be yours."
I proposed to her finally, and to my surprise, she was already committed. I didn't give up.

I tried my best, bent heaven and hell to convince her, and things started going outright.
We talked, became close friends, and two years passed.
Some misunderstandings started popping up after I met her and her friends on a college trip to my city Jodhpur.
From there, she said things which, cannot be revoked.
More than 200 messages, 50 calls, and all went in vain.
That's where I broke all ties, and the darkness took over once again.

SHADES OF PINK

The light was faint, but her light pink, matte-finished lipstick was apparent to me.
"That lipstick looks nice," I said, sipping my wine.
With a surprising look on her face as she sipped her wine, she said, "quite an observer, but thanks for the compliment."
Her lips had the precise shape and, the way she smiled was giving me bolts of shocks.
Just as the wine from her glass touched her lips,
The hue left behind was something very different.
Her lipstick had a look that complimented her personality.
Just as she looked Stunning, gorgeous, and damn hot, her lipstick was dark, full of suspense yet breathe taking.

I was so lost and, it was so evident that she said suddenly, "you should stop staring at my lips and instead make a move for it."
I looked up and, she smiled as she pulled her hairs to the back of her ears.
Candles have something magical about them.
Either they create suspense or they create Romance. In my case, the latter was much more prominent.
Candle Light helps comfort two people meeting for the first time and helps relax the air of hesitation around them.
I sat there staring at her, and she was sitting right across

the table.
Words were less but, still, our glances exchanged a thousand words.

"Want to go on to the rooftop"? I asked. "It's too many people here."
"Sure," she said and smiled as I held out my hand and helped her get up.
The rooftop was much more peaceful and, with the cold wind blowing, it was even more satisfying.

I stood near the railing with her hand resting on mine. Our eyes, capturing the beauty of the lake and the necklace of drive-in areas surrounding it.

The winds blew fast and, her hand slipped in mine, hugging it tightly to avoid the cold winds.
Just as I turned towards her, as I took off my coat and covered her with it to protect her from those chilly winds, her hands slipped onto my neck and hugged me tightly.

Her cold yet soft hands felt like velvet running on my skin.
I was too surprised to move and, the scent of her Musk perfume was soothing enough to make my head rest upon her shoulders as her fingers ran in my hairs.
I reciprocated the hug and felt our beats synchronize with every passing minute.

THE LAKE-SIDE RESTRO

I sat in the Lakeside restaurant peeping around, waiting for my order, when my eyes stopped on her. It seemed as if my neck refused to move, and my eyes went on a hang mode while I took a sip of my wine from my glass. I was the only person sitting all by myself in that noisy and busy place where people were having fun, mostly with their friends.

She was sitting right across a couple of tables, and as luck would have been, her face was partially visible, which forced me to imagine the other half of it on my own.

I grew more impatient as her voice penetrated my eyes, sending a spark of curiosity down my spine just as I was about to start writing. I realized that my mind was still picturing her, and the story I was thinking of was nowhere near remembrance in my mind.

So, I turned towards her, took a casual glance. However, her eyes were already staring at me for a good couple of seconds before passing a smile which suddenly brought me back to my senses.

She had something unusual about her. Those eyes, pinning on you as if they want to force you down and so mesmerizing that you will not even mind them doing so.

I acted as if I was still writing and concentrating on my

laptop. (it's the best I could do to hide my smile). My mind decided to go with the flow and carve out a story with the best I could think because those eyes had that charm to imprint that looks in anyone's eyes and forces them to think of, even if it was for a split second.

I wished I dared to go and talk to her, especially when she smiled. I was trying hard not to look at her because I knew she was looking at me from time to time and, I could feel it. But curiosity gets the better of us every damn time, and I took the step raising my head towards her, where she was busy talking to her friends but looking at me occasionally from the corner of her eyes and finally turned towards me.

This time I did not pull away from her eyes because either it would go right or she might ignore it, which was the worst of all that could happen. I waved my hand at her lifting it from my keyboard where my fingers were busy working on the keys.

I was not expecting any response, but to my surprise, she too waived in my direction. I looked back to see and make sure that she was not waving at anyone else, but when I turned towards her, with a burst of controlled laughter, she pointed to me with a message that she was waving to me only. I gave a smile and sat back, relaxed on my chair.

Mind if I give you some company, Mr.? she said and stopped.

Rahul, I said, getting up from my chair.

Nikita, she replied with her hand extended forward.

I shook her hand, and damn, they felt as if I was holding a ball of cotton.

Shall I? She asked.

With pleasure, I remarked and signalling her friends to continue with their dinner informed that she would stay with me for a while.
Would you like something I asked her as she took her seat comfortably?

Umm, Honestly, I had my drinks but, I sure am in a mood For a long drive, She said with a smile as her eyes avoided contact with me.

It appeared as if I was dreaming, and it took me back to some of the precious moments that my stories had in them. Although fictional, they were mine but, this at present was what I had been dreaming of for eternity.

THE METRO GIRL - PART 1

It's 9 AM & I am standing in the metro, on my way to my office just like any other day and, so is everyone else. Standing near the door, I peek outside from the windows on the door, watching the world move backward as the train accelerates forward.

As the train Slows down, the view is interrupted by another train on the adjoining track. It stops, and my eyes catch hold of that girl, near the door, with a pair of specs on those deep brown eyes, Hairs flowing down her face, covering her face partially.

From a frown on my face because of the sudden interruption, my heart skips a beat. Those flicks make their way onto her face repeatedly as if trying to conceal her from my vision tempting my curiosity to have one small peek at her.

With a realization of a comparatively long-stop, she looks up suddenly only to find me staring at her. Our eyes meet, and I try to raise my hand to wave at her, but the gesture comes from her side first.

With a mechanical error in place and some time in hand, we both initiate our introduction via sign language.

I try my best, but she seems like a pro in it.

The train is about to move and, before I can think of

something, she turns her phone towards me with her number written on it.

She asks me to copy it.
Just as we finish, the train departs and, we move in opposite directions to our destinations.
Reaching my station, I check my phone, and there is a text from her.
"Hi, It's Nisha here. Just a small information for you to know that I can't speak."
I text back- " since when has a conversation between two people been dependent on talking"?
She replies with a smile.

THE METRO GIRL - PART 2

It had been a couple of months or so after I met Nisha on a metro in Delhi.

She had something that dragged me towards her. That aura was magical. We started with chats, and slowly when the comfort level started to match, we started sharing pictures on WhatsApp ranging from breakfast, lunch to boss giving a presentation at the conference.

We had a compatibility that was surprising for both of us. From caring to scolding and playlists to movies, we shared it all.

I texted her, "Would you like to have a video call"?

She was busy or maybe skeptical because she read the message but didn't reply.

It was late in the evening when my screen flashed a new message from her.

It read-

"Rahul, I am not sure about a video call because it makes me uncomfortable every time I realize that I am not normal, I can't talk to you, and it feels weird."

It's fine. I understand your concern & I won't force you for anything. I texted back and got back to work.

There is a saying that if you give time, things fall in place on their own without much hard work, provided your intentions are in the right place.

Around midnight, when I was taking my dinner (which is usually late) & busy working on my book, My phone rang. I reached out to grab my phone, and I was in for a surprise.

She was there in front of me, waiting for me to answer the call.
Swiping up, I answered her call, and the smile on her face was priceless.
She asked me to wait for a minute and went away to grab something from her desk.
They were something like small placards, but I could not make out what was on them.
I asked, " what are you hiding"?
In reply, she displayed a placard that read "A surprise for you."
Oh, I said and closed my work, turned towards the camera to see what she had to show.

She changed the placard, and the 2nd one read -
" Although I can't speak, you still make me feel comfortable and normal."

I could not help but smile, and she was blushing at the same time as her curls half hid her smile.
That feeling made me feel special, and my heart was racing like never before.

My eyes were locked in her face when she changed the placard, and this one was something he had never

expected.
It read - *"You made me realize that it only takes a caring person to share this life. Your caring nature and utmost understanding attitude have made my heart fall for you"*.
Her final placard read -
" Will you go on a date with me"?
All I could do was nod in agreement with her proposal.
Words should never limit how much you love your partner.

A FACE IN HAZE

Her Face was a bit indistinct, but It felt as if I knew her already. Sitting in front of her, I could not make out who she was, although it felt like someone very close to me.
She had that air of uncertainty perfectly blended with Romance, just like sugar dissolved in a glass of lemonade.
"Who are you?" I asked her in a confused tone.
She giggled and replied, "I don't see the zeal inside you, Rahul, to find out who I am."
My sanity was racing in all directions to figure out who she was, but something was making me nervous. Maybe it was her chuckle or, it was the silence we sat in, or it was the cold gusts.
It felt like an eternity while sitting in front of her, still with no clues on who she was.
"Still no answer"? she asked and walked up to me.
I sat they transfixed as she came close to me, and the aroma of her Rosemary perfume surrounded me. Suddenly, I heard an alarm sound, and she grinned.

" Maybe later, sweety she said, and I was startled as I woke up to my phone alarm sounding near my ears.
I sat there, all drenched in sweat and nothing but a distinct hum from the ceiling fan that was pretty much the only sound and me the only person in the room.

Thinking of it as a dream, I kept my phone away and was about to sleep when I felt a small piece of paper near my head.

It appeared as if it had something written on it.

Turning on the flashlight on my phone, I opened it up to see what it was.

On it, in beautiful writing was-

"Maybe, later sweety".

THE ROAD LESS TAKEN

An Admirable choice for a book, He said suddenly.

She looked up to find a guy in his early 20's, holding a camera in his hand while still shivering in the crisp winter mornings of Italy.

"I guess so," she replied. "Just started it, no idea as of now."

Oh, ok, he said, and then there was an awkward silence. Neither of them said anything for quite a while. So finally bringing up Courage and Breaking the ice, he said "Hi, I am Jay"

She looked at him for a minute, and as he was about to draw his hand back, she extended hers.

"Meera", she said. Nice to meet you.

"Pleasure is all mine", he replied.

"May I"...?he asked, pointing towards the chair.

She shifted a bit, and he sat down.

"How come here? She asked. I mean, not many people come here to click pictures alone, at least.

Jay smiled and said, "Well, I like it here. It's peaceful and calm". As far as someone is concerned, I'm all alone here in Italy.

"I see," She said and turned away. Did she smile?....maybe Jay was imagining.

"Do you like to read"? she asked, adjusting her specs.

"Why do you think so"? Jay questioned back.

"You seem to have good knowledge about trending books in the market, like this one", he said, pointing towards the one she was reading.

Jay smiled and said, "No, I am not that much of a reader, but I am more into writing.

Do you write? Books? or something? She asked, looking surprised.

"Well, I have launched a book, it's new in-market let's see how it goes", he said.

"Well", she said, "let me know the name. I'll give you an unbiased review."

Jay smiled and, picking up the book she was reading, handed it over to her.

She was stunned. She looked up, confused, and then crosschecked the author's name, clearly written JAY MALHOTRA.

"God! you are the author?"......and you said it's new she said surprisingly.

"I have read many of your works and I love them," she said, while talking, scuffled through her bag searching for something.

"What are you looking for"? He asked.

"Well, I'll need an autograph on this book", and Jay handed over the signed book to her even before she could ask.

"Now that you have a gift, would you mind giving me something?" he asked hesitantly.

"Depends on what you ask," she said with a smile.

Nothing too big, Jay said, just a walk in this silent woody path and lunch together?

She blushed and said, "Yes, sounds good to me."

TEA OVER BEER

A tiring day at work was enough for me to be frustrated. The cold winds howling outside the Lounge did nothing more than add fuel to the fire. I sat there, sipping my tea, watching my beautiful ride standing outside when someone interrupted the view.

I looked up to see who it was.

Standing in front of me was a girl sporting a black leather jacket on denim jeans, with a pair of spectacles adding to her features.

May I? she asked, pointing towards the chair in front of me.

Sure, I said.

Thanks, she said and smiled back. I thought she might take the chair But, to my surprise, she sat right in front of me.

I sat there without uttering a single word and was soon busy with my laptop when she suddenly broke the silence.

Working? She asked.

I looked up and saw her trying to take a peek at my laptop.

Na, just some random stuff, I said as I closed it.

Tough day at work, I guess? She asked.

Yeah, kind of off. I replied. How did you guess?

Well, she checked me out from top to bottom and said, a perfectly well-dressed man, maybe straight from the office, sitting in a lounge, having tea rather than a beer, and working on some random stuff, I guess that makes it easy

and leaned back.
Interesting. I said, sipping my tea which was already cold by that time.
There was silence for a split second, and then she broke the ice between us.
So, where do you work? She asked.
Currently, I am working for a fashion brand as a senior executive. I said.
Fashion business? That's amazing, She said, All excited.
We NIFTian's have a different life. I said.
NIFT? She exclaimed. Damn, that's a place where one dreams to be life must have been Amazing there.
Not exactly. I replied and ordered another cup of tea.
What you see is just the tip of the iceberg, I said. What the reality is, hides deep down the roots.
What does this mean? She asked, leaning forward, as her interest increased in my talks.
Nothing, I said, leave that and smiled.

By the way, I am Poorva. she said as she extended her hand.
Rahul, I said, extending mine.
So, where do you work? I asked her.
"I have just completed my BBA and currently working in an advertising agency."

So, the fashion industry must be introducing to a lot of different people. She asked.
Yeah, and that too pretty damn extreme variety of people.
Are you Dating anyone? She asked.
This question took me by surprise, and I almost choked on my tea.

Ummm. Not really into dating, I replied, clearing my throat and avoiding eye contact for some time.
Searching for your soul mate or just not into dating anyone right now?
Well, things have not exactly turned out very good for me, so you can say that I am at peace right now.
What about you? I asked her, trying to stay calm at the same time.
She leaned back and smiled. I kept looking at her questioningly as I took another sip of my tea.
Well, I am waiting for someone with whom I can feel safe, homely, share everything and be more of friends rather than just two people in a relationship.

Matching thoughts, I must admit I said. Although it's tough these days, old-school people still are the same. Right? Well, that's surprising, she said.
I gave her a questioning look.
Honestly, looking at you, no one can imagine you saying that she said, and I leaned forward. I think she understood the step.
I mean, a well-dressed man, looks good, has an attitude that does attract girls, and owns a perfect ride. You are a complete package for any girl. She said, with her hands raised.
That was it a compliment? I asked at last.
Of course, it was, She replied with a smile.
"You don't like compliments?"
Nothing like that, I replied. By the way, thanks.

She had something about herself that attracted me to her. You are going mad, I said to myself and tried to control

my mind that was going in that way, which I have always stopped from wandering in.
Lost in my World, a loud ringing sound brought me back to reality.
It was her phone ringing.
Looking at her phone, she said, "maybe I'll see you around?" and smiled.
Even before I could reconstruct what she said, she was gone.
Will we ever meet again? I thought.

I finished my tea, and my mind again wandered away somewhere, thinking about her.
Just then, the waiter handed me a piece of paper, along with the Bill.
A lady left it for you, told me to hand it over to you as you left.
I flipped it open and read.

"Well, ... how about another cup of tea together?
8 P.M. TOMORROW. DON'T BE LATE.
- POORVA

And all I could do was smile, as I rode back home, with the winds which were annoying me some time back,
blowing straight on my face, and believe me, it felt amazing.

BACK FOR YOU

Now you are far away, she said with hands on her hips and her eyes stern, still craving for a hug from him.
He was speechless as She stood there and believing his eyes was something too much to take at once.
The suitcase stood by her side, which she was supposed to take and be off with her fiancé.

Either his drink was too Hard, or he was hallucinating because it was impossible to be true.
Hey, do you see that girl standing there? He asked the man sitting beside him.
He ignored his question and resumed his drink.
She walked up to him and came up close enough where he could smell her perfume and feel her breathe.
You were on a flight to Dubai. I guess he said, still trying to balance himself.
What are you doing here? I don't deserve you.

Tears rolled down her eyes, seeing him like this.
Pulling him towards herself, she burst into years. Everyone was surprised as he stood still transfixed, and all she managed to say was, "I am sorry."

"It took me a bit too long to realize that I still love you, and living without you is not worth it," she said. "I committed a mistake leaving you that time when you needed me the most. I don't want to repeat it".

He pulled himself together and, holding her face in his hand, said - "I am never letting you go now."

BONDED WITH LOVE

My head rested peacefully on her lap as her hands moved through my hairs and those warm lips planted a kiss on my lips.
Although I was looking upside down, Her smile was still looking beautiful, and my stare made her question me.
"what are you staring at?"
"Well, I was trying to understand how I got lucky enough to get you by my side," I said, trying to get up, but she pushed me down.
"You are not getting up," she said. "I like it this way, and as far as getting me is a concern, I don't have words to tell you what do you mean to me."

I smiled as her soft cotton-like hands encompassed my face, and she gave me a tight hug.
"I never thought I would ever be able to love someone," she said, "but you entered my life, and everything changed."

She was the best thing to ever happen in my life, and having her by my side was my record achievement ever.

SOME FINAL WORDS

She texted - "Do you miss me?"
He responded - "what do you want me to say?"
She said - "The truth."
He paused for a moment, and she could see the blue tick on her end but the wait for a reply seemed like an eternity.
A text popped up, and she was left speechless.
"I don't want to, yet I miss you, but with time, I have learned to ignore the fact, and honestly, now I don't care if my heart misses you, my emotions have moved on, and they usually don't turn around."
A droplet of tear left her eyes unsaid and untold as she read -
"You can't respond to this conversation anymore."

Sometimes the fact that we still miss them is deeply embedded in our emotions. We need to make sure that the wounds inflicted once should be left behind so as not to evoke a sense of pain

River of emotions as it flows never goes back stream, and we should not try to mend things that are a part of a long lost past.

WHEN WE MET

"Love knows no language. It's a language in itself. Words often fall short to explain what we feel for someone who means a lot more than they know."

My write-up was good, and the crowd in the open mic was listening with a smile which boosted my confidence.

A regular, single guy talking about love was something that connected with people who had more or less experienced the same.

Letting things go is hard when you realize that they won't be coming to you. No matter how hard you try because mutual feelings are necessary to make a connection. So, till you find someone who connects with you, keep your hopes up and the love inside you alive.

My write-up ended with applause and a cheer from the crowd in the cafe.

Taking a seat near the bar, I ordered a drink before getting engrossed listening to others.
I didn't notice someone taking a seat beside me until a

small "excuse me" brought me to my senses as I looked back, only to be surprised by a girl sitting just next to me.

Short Hair flowing up to her shoulders and her hands encompassing a glass which was pretty much fresh.
A dark blue velvet dress added up to her looks, and those eyes prevented me from saying something for a couple of seconds.

"Umm, hi". I said, getting myself together.
"Ria", she said, extending her hand.
"RV," I said, shaking hands.
"And that's the name?" she asked curiously.
I gave a smile at her comment and said," Rahul."
"Heard you speak a few minutes back she said. I was overwhelmed by that small write-up of yours."
"I am...glad". I said, a bit surprised.

"We saw you all secluded, and we thought if you would like to join us over there", she said, Looking to a table where her friends were looking at us.
I don't know if that will be fine, I said with a bit of hesitation.
"We'll be glad," she said as she got up and signaled me to walk along.

Maybe it was just the timing, or it was a signal, but the speakers played *"Perfect"* by Ed Sheeran, and it struck me differently.

I don't know if it was only me who noticed, but her smile

and the blush on her alight pink cheeks gave it out that she too was listening, and it did strike her too.

THE DREAM

The noise was too loud, almost as if someone was using a drill machine in his head. He craned his head to relieve the cramp in his neck. When he couldn't move, he realized where he was in a coffin deep in the confines of an aeroplane.
The suffocating air, the closed space, was getting uneasy with every passing minute.

The sound could still be heard, but try as much he could not move.

A tingling sensation slowly encompassed his entire body, and a faint beep was audible, but he was too Drowsy to see anything.
She came running to the room only to find him shivering helplessly in his sleep.

The sleep paralysis accompanied by the horrors of the Army massacre made his sleep a nightmare hard to forget.
But she was always there, and he could feel it.
The vitals on the monitors was soon back to normal as her lips kissed his head.

DRIVE TO HOME

Corporate life sucks. It turns your life into a living hell no matter what you do. I said as the waitress laid my drinks on the table.

You have no idea what we go through, she said and smiled, enjoy your drinks, and walked away.

I watched her as she walked away and disappeared into the crowd. Whatever I said to myself and then turning to my table poured my scotch in the sexy-looking glass and was busy admiring its beauty when a familiar voice interrupted my thought process. It tastes best when chilled. Said a voice, and I turned around to find the same waitress standing behind me. It was then that I realized that not only it had been quite some time that I was observing the glass so closely that I forgot to put some ice in it.

Oh yeah, I was lost. You know. I said, straightening myself a bit.

She gave a small smile and then went away.

By the time I finished, it was 11 P.M., I got up, put my coat on, and was inside my car, which felt like a comfy heater on that cold night.

Just as I was about to leave, I saw someone standing near the bus stand in a black one-piece looking around for some conveyance or maybe waiting for someone. Although not drunk, I was tipsy, and it was difficult to

identify who it was from that distance.
I drove over and found that she was the same waitress who served me in the evening. I stopped my car and got out, it was cold outside, and the chilled breeze made it even worse.

Hey, I said waiting for someone?
Oh, hey, she said. I was hoping to find an e- rickshaw that might drop me home.
That might be tough at this point. I replied.
She just shrugged her shoulders in reply, and there was a brief silence between us. Can I drop you home if you want? One could tell it from her look that she was not sure about it, and before she said anything, I said, I am neither drunk or have any bad intentions. You can call at your home and tell them that a friend is dropping you by if you want, I said. That would not be necessary. she said. I think I can trust you on that and gave that smile again. If you please, I said as I opened the door.
Thank you, she said.

I never thought that this ride would change my life forever and that too in such a way that I could never have imagined.
Five minutes later, we were rolling on the main road. So, where should I drop you? I asked. I live in Dwarka, she said slowly. Hey, relax. I said.
I will drop you wherever you wish, ok? We drove in silence for a while, and then she broke the ice finally.
Well, it is awkward that you are helping me, and we still have not introduced ourselves. I am Sanjana she said.
Rahul, I replied, sensing her next question. I work as a

senior photographer for a fashion magazine.
That sounds interesting, she said. It looks like a fascinating job.

It is more of a dream come true, which I had since my college days in NIFT.
Quiet formally dressed for a fashion student, she replied.
We both laughed. Yes, that is something I love to do.
Anyways, what about you? I asked. I noticed her smile fade away into a dull expression.
It is ok if you are not comfortable. I said. And with that, I turned up the volume on my music system playing EVERYTHING I DO by Bryan Adams.
She turned down the volume and said, I was in college doing my BA from DU when my father passed away, and our family ran into financial crises. Being the eldest of the siblings had to drop my college in my 3rd year and take up a job to support my family and pay the fees for my sisters. It has been five years now, and everything is the same.

I overheard her in silence and kept quiet even when she finished.
I would not say that I understand your situation because I have never been in one of them, but I can say that if there is darkness, light does dawn upon there sooner or later, I replied. She was surprised at my remark as I saw it. That was comforting to be true. She replied. Most people only say that they know how they feel just for the sake of it, even when they have no idea about it.
Thank you for being honest, she replied.
The atmosphere changed from a serious one to a bit friendly one.

So I decided to continue that way. So, what are your hobbies? I asked Maybe, something you love to do in your free time?.

Do you seriously think I have time for hobbies in this busy life? She enquired. Why not? I exclaimed, there are things that we do in our free time. Come on.

She was about to say something when I interrupted.

Spill it, and instead of telling me, burst out in laughter.

Yes, I write a bit, whenever I am free, She replied.

Do you write? I asked in astonishment.

Maybe I can give you some extra motivation by telling you that I might be able to help you publish some of your works if you have something nice in-store.

Are you serious? That would be a great favor. she squealed.

Don't call it a favor, please, consider it a little help from my side as a friend. I said and smiled.

She did not say a word but just smiled, pulled her flicks to the back of her ears, and she looked beautiful while doing that. I had to admit.

Our destination was still a long way, and we sat in silence for some time. I deliberately slowed down my speed without her noticing because somewhere inside, I was enjoying her company.

Mind if I ask you something? I said, turning towards her.

Yeah, sure, go on. she said as she turned herself a bit towards me. I am not sure if I should ask you this but, what is your perception about relationships, I said without looking at her.

See, I have no perceptions about relationships, she said in a different tone.

I felt that I just offended her, but before I could even say anything, she interrupted, but you can directly ask me if I am dating someone or not and, started laughing, looking at the color of my face change.

You got scared, she enquired, still laughing.

Obviously yes. I responded, recovering from the shock because it is not every day that I talk to girls or share a nice late-night drive with them. I am a loner, you can say.

Oh, come on, you are in the fashion business, and you say you do not interact with girls? She said sarcastically.

Believe it or not, this is what it is. I said in a deep voice.

What is what it is? She asked.

I replied Being in the fashion business does not mean that I interact with girls privately. It is pure business to me.

She kept quiet for some time and then said I want to ask you something too.

Yeah sure. I replied. How many girls have you dated? She asked

One, I replied. During my school life and that too was one-sided, so we broke up a few months later. She gave me a look like she did hear something unbelievable.

What? I questioned, looking at her.

Her look gave me a weird feeling.

Please stop staring like that.

Are you telling me that in your entire life, you never had a relationship? She asked me in a high-pitched shocking tone.

What makes you think that I will lie to you about it? I questioned her.

And to avoid her questions, I turned up the volume of my music system, but she turned it down once again and said,

I sense something inside you, Rahul, something that you have kept to yourself for so long that now it shows on your face.

Fine, if you want to know. I replied.
It is not like I never tried dating anyone, or I did not have any crushes in my school life or college, but every time I approached someone, it ended up in rejection, and every time it just broke my confidence from inside. It made me believe that I was not the kind of person that any girl would want me as their partner, and after facing so many rejections, I decided not to think about it anymore and focus on what I want to do in my life.
Living alone is a sort of habit for me.
I am seriously sorry, she said in a soft tone. I should have never asked you to talk about it.
I replied in a dull tone, you were right. I have carried it way too long inside me, and that might be the reason I was overprotective about it.
I can not even imagine being in your place and be strong enough to face it all, She said, sliding back in the chair.

It was midnight, and I was feeling hungry, and it came to my mind that I skipped my meal.
Sanjana might have skipped it too.
Are you hungry even a bit? I asked because I am feeling damn hungry.
I am. she replied. But, I will have something when I get back home.
I knew she was hungry and why she was reluctant to eat outside.
So without asking her, I spotted a restaurant and stopped

my car over there.
Come on, I said. Let us eat something.
She was reluctant.

Oh, come on, I Said, dinner is on me, and stop treating me like a stranger. Although we are but still, I can at least do this and stretched my hand out. She took my hand and came out of the car.
We sat on our seats, eyes fixed on her and hers spying around the place.
This place looks expensive she said, can we go somewhere else?
Will a Dhabha do for you? I asked.
That sounds more like me she smiled.
We left the restaurant and, in a few minutes, found ourselves in a Desi dhabha.
Sanjana looked quite comfortable out here. She not only ordered for herself but also placed an order for me.

Trust me, She said. You are going to love the food here. We both had a great time during dinner, and as the dhabha was about to close, we decided to continue our journey as it was late already.
This journey was getting better every minute, and I did not want to accept it, but also it is a fact which I could not deny. It was a feeling like this journey should continue more than just one night.
So, she said suddenly, which brought me back to the real world once again.
Tell me why a person like you is always out at the bar all alone?
Why? I enquired, can someone not be with themselves for

some time? Then it struck me, wait a minute, you just said is always out alone?

Yeah, she answered casually. I did see you a couple of times there, but my services were not available to you at that time. She said and gave me an eye-to-eye look, and talking about you being alone, I must say, you are honest, a gentleman and clapped, also as far as being humble is concerned I don't have words for you, but you are just perfect.

Well, Honestly, I said, your company did make my day better.
I am seriously going to remember this day.
You are going to remember this day, and what about me? She asked in a soft voice without looking at me.
I looked at her once, and she turned at the same time. It did become an awkward moment for me, but then I somehow got my shit together and said, I can not imagine remembering this day without remembering you.

We both stared at each other, and I could see in the dim street lights that she was blushing, and so was I.
Suddenly then out of nowhere, she came forward and was about to kiss me when suddenly the girl in the GPS interrupted in between - you have arrived at the destination, and I saw her retreating with closed eyes.
So, finally, you are home. I said.

Yeah, all thanks to you. she replied.
Had you not been there today, it would have been a big problem for me. I got out of the car and opened her gate.

She took my hand and stepped out.
So, it was nice meeting you. I said as I brought my hand forward.
She accepted the handshake, and we felt something when we shook hands. Neither did she leave my hand, nor did I.
Suddenly realizing it, I released her hand.
So, I hope I will see you around sometime. I said with a cheerful voice.
Yeah, sure, She said softly. Thanks for today, Rahul. It was great meeting you.
My pleasure, I replied with a smile and then turned around to sit in my car.
She suddenly pulled me towards her and locked her lips with mine. I was dumbstruck then. Everything just seemed to fade away, and I felt her hands go around my neck as she came closer every minute.

She parted her lips from mine, and I looked at her, eyes still closed and breathing heavily.
We stood there so close that we could feel our heartbeat sync in rhythm. That was a feeling which had no words to express how I felt.

You loved the ride today? she asked me, still panting heavily.
That was the best night ride I ever had in the first place, I replied.
I would never do it to anyone But, you have something different which attracts me to you.
You bring a smile on my face, she said.
I gave her a confused look because this type of encounter was new to someone like me. She came closer to me,

holding my collar, pulled me towards herself.
My heart was still racing.
What I want to say is that I want to have this type of night ride with you all my life, and every night we spend can be better than the previous one.

I held her by her waist and pulled her closer to me, and planted a kiss on her lips. She responded passionately, not realizing that we were there on the road, kissing for time unknown. So, if you are free tomorrow, she said, let us admire a couple of wine glasses over dinner?
Oh! So, am I being asked out? Like seriously? I said in a surprised voice.

Be there at 8:00 P.M., Marcos Club tomorrow. She said, and finally giving me a peck on my cheeks, she smiled and walked away.
Watching her walk away, I had some thoughts in my mind. My whole life, I was searching for a partner whom I could bond with, who could have thought that something as random as this would change my life for years to come.
Writing this today, I still remember that day when I first met her.
How lucky I am to have her with me.

You do not find love. Love finds you.

MATTER OF TIME

Seven years is a long time for realizing something. Maybe yes, maybe not. As people say, it is never too late, but honestly, you never know.

A message popped up today from someone whom I least expected to remember me. Whose memories were somewhat distant and faded.
The feelings at this point are somewhat mixed and confusing.
The contact, although, was not saved on my phone. But, the DP with a smiling face, flaunting a Pink skirt was enough for me to identify my first crush.
With flashbacks running through my mind and a dilemma whether to reply immediately or should not, I sat there hovering my hands over the highlighted chat on my screen.
Suddenly a couple of more messages popped up from her side. Unintentionally, I clicked it open.

The silence of seven years between our last chat, the awkwardness between us was a matter of concern. But nothing of that sort was evident from the messages and, they were no small talks.
Except for a small Hi Rahul, her texts were long.

I could feel my heartthrob with such a force that it felt like exploding.
Sliding my work aside, and with a thousand questions running in my mind, I took my seat on the recliner in my balcony and read out what she had to say.

Hi Rahul.
It has been a long time. How have you been?
I know you have some questions, and even I was skeptical messaging you but sometimes talking to someone you know feels much more comfortable, even if it is after a long time.

I know my sudden message might bring uploads of old forgotten memories, and I can imagine the look on your face right now but, I needed someone to talk, someone close.

It might be possible that you have moved on with your life.
I don't want to intrude in again, but sometimes when things are not right, we need someone. Am I selfish? Maybe yes, but also helpless.

Reply if you feel like you can keep aside everything I did, including my mistakes.

I was confused like never before and sat back in my chair, rocking to and fro. My mind was so lost in thoughts that I did not even notice Blacky, the cute labra that I had, walk up to me before she placed her head on my lap.

She was the one who always knew somehow when I was tensed and was always ready to cuddle on my lap.

Sometimes, how things get back to you and how life sticks your past right in your face when everything is going smooth were some of the thoughts that jumped across my mind.

Blacky was the one I used to talk to whenever I had a tough time. She looked at me as I said - Do you remember Priya? She wagged her tail as if understanding my words and then turned towards my phone, where the chat was still open, gave a woof!
I kissed her forehead, and another message popped up from her side.

I know you are reading this and are confused, whether to reply or not. It is understandable, and I will be fine with whatever you decide.

It is true that once you love someone, you can not unlove them, but you can find someone, whom you love even more, but in my case, the second part was nearly non-existent, and the first one was a truth hard to accept.
Hi, I texted back after much consideration, and within seconds, I could see her typing something.
I guess she was a bit taken aback because the Reply I got was a blank emoji.
Which was followed by a message -
How are you?

I have never been better all these years. I replied.
It has been a long time. She texted back.
Seven years, seven months & fifteen days, to be precise. I replied.

There was a momentary pause between her reading the message and replying.

You counted it from that day!?, her message conveyed the surprise in her voice.

Forgetting such a day is not easy for anyone. I replied.
The worst feeling is experiencing Love and Hatred for the same person with the same intensity.
The craving that wants them back so bad, but at the same time, your conscious reminds you of the past that you have tried to leave behind, but even the slightest of remembrance is nothing less than a painful sting.
That insulting rejection seven years back still was afresh in my mind, just like it happened yesterday.

The sound of the slap echoing throughout the corridor made heads turn around, but all I did was smile and said - A simple no would have been enough, and walked away, without turning back, trying to hide my tears which although left my eyes but never touched the ground.

That was the day I realized that looks never justify your personality and attitude. She had a smile to kill but the rudeness and pride that she carried overshadowed everything, and that was one of the reasons she had no friends in the college.

I landed back into reality from the flashbacks when Blacky nudged at my hand, looking towards my phone.

I looked at it, and there was a voice note from her side, and as her habit was to speak very fast. I knew she had a lot many things to say in there.

Let me not bore you with the details of the voice note that was a mixture of many things, and to my surprise, the originally hyper Priya sounded calm and composed, but not happy, that I could surely sense.
Sometimes history repeats itself, or you can say that fate provides you with another chance to make things work out in a way you always wanted.

For me, it was something I never thought would happen to me & the smile hiding behind that tensed face was the sign of feelings arising again from scratch.

Still there? She texted back.

Love knows no bounds and when you get a chance to rewrite your future with someone you have always dreamt of, never let go.

I always have been. I texted back and received a pumping heart emoji with a blank emoji.

I will call you in a minute. I texted back to the sweet blank emoji.

Ummm, you should walk down your flat to the lawn in the front, She texted back.

This text got my heart racing again & I was more surprised than speechless.
Without replying to that text and clad in my pajama, I rushed down to the lawn.
Only to find someone pacing up and down the path between the lawn.

Meeting her after seven years was like a dream, and believing her to be standing there for real, was even more difficult.
Standing there in front of me was Priya, flaunting a pair of heels, blue denim shorts, and a black crop top. Her eyes were still light brown but captivating enough to hold you at your place.

Our eyes met, and a smile passed from both sides. It took my eyes some time to adjust to the darkness and the dim yellow light glowing a few feet away, But my girl was already in focus, and nothing else mattered to me.

She walked towards me in short slow steps, Hairs flowing with that monsoon wind and that sharp cut jawline visible in the street light.

Everything came to a standstill as we stood face to face, her hands fidgeting and my hands in my pocket with shoulders shrugged up, trying to shield myself from the winds.

Hi, she said, Finally breaking the ice.
Hello. I replied.
It had been a long time since I met her, and the hyper girl I knew was now more calm and composed. Also, she was bold and never shied away from doing what she wanted.
She never was the small talk person, and before I could say anything or even had the idea of shaking hands, I found myself entangled in her arms. As her hands slid slowly from my shoulder to my neck and her grip grew tighter as she advanced closer.

My hands were still in my pocket, reluctant to reach out and hold her like the way she was doing. She sensed the reluctance and, pulling my hands out, slid them on her waist.
My eyes were, fixed on her, and she stared right back at me. As if asking something.

I shook my head, trying to avoid the question that was about to pop up from her side when she pulled my face towards herself and said in a low voice.
What happened? Why do you look kind of......,
before she could complete her sentence? I said, Confused.
Precisely, she said.

Yes, I was a bit surprised, somewhat happy, somewhat confused. Everything was just a mix-up, and it was getting difficult to separate every feeling from the other one.

What changed? I asked her finally.

The smile had faded away a bit as she pulled me close, and her face rested on my shoulders.
Her hairs had a fragrance of Night-blooming Jasmin, and I could feel them on my face as the winds blew.
Maybe it was a feeling of comfort, or it was something else.
I felt a drop of tear run down my right shoulder and a soft sob from her.
I was a bit surprised because this side of her was something unknown to me and maybe everyone else who had known her.
Nothing changed, She said.
I held her face in my hands and wiped off those tears that, although had left her eyes but refused to let go of her soft peach-colored cheeks.

After we graduated, my relationship with Vinod changed. Things went from bad to worse. We tried fixing things up, but every time it ended up in a fight. I tried to ignore many things, but he would mess up every time.
He cheated on you, I said with a voice of certainty, and she nodded in agreement.
He cheated on me for one whole year and then suddenly left.
Saying this, she broke down.
That was the day I realized that what he had for me was mere attraction and what you had was love. He wanted my body. You just wanted me.
His interest in me deteriorated with time as he found someone better than me while you still are here even after seven long years.

She avoided eye contact but continued speaking-'maybe you have already moved on in your life and forgotten me but, she stopped and looked at me.
I looked at her expectantly, signaling her to complete her sentence.
If you have a space available in your heart to accept me back in your life, I would like to stay there forever. She said and smiled in the most minimalistic manner that made my heart skip a beat.

What happened seven years back was something I was ready to forgive to have her back in my life because fate had put me in a spot, from where everything looked just perfect, and the missing piece that I was searching for so long was now in front of me.

That girl stood in front of me with her hand in mine. She looked at me as I held her hands up and planted a kiss on her fingers.

I have always been there, You took a bit too long to recognize me, but now that you are here, I am not letting you go, I said as tears rolled down my eyes.
Hearing this, she pulled me towards herself and hugged me tightly, completely embracing me in her hold.
Let us go home? I asked her as she stood there, still holding me in her arms.
I want to stay with you tonight. She said In a low voice which clutching my shirt in those fists.

I smiled as her puppy face came up, which was her counter to any argument she wanted to win.

That is the home I am talking about, I said as I pulled her cheeks, and she blushed.

As I walked home with her hand in mine, the world changed for me. It became more vibrant, more hopeful, and more lively.

Blacky sat there beside the doorway, peeking on us and wagging her tail.
Woof! she shouted, grabbing Priya's attention.
I see you have an adorable partner she said as her she patted her head.

Blacky was already loving her.
Yes, I replied, and she has something to say.
Really? she asked, looking at me, trying to hide a smile that was almost evident on her face.

Welcome home, I said. Pushing those flicks to the back of those ears as her hands pulled me close.
Her lips left a mark on my neck.

My life took a turn with Priya coming in again. Something was missing from my life, and after four failed relationships all these years, I realized that my feelings for Priya never gave up.

Today writing this with her head resting on my shoulders and hands holding me tightly, I know what it feels like to be with someone you always wanted to be a part of your life.

www.ingramcontent.com/pod-product-compliance
Lightning Source LLC
LaVergne TN
LVHW100337181026
850499LV00039B/1115